Great Aunt Rowena sniffed, looking down her nose at Dominic. But then she caught sight of the Topper on his head. Her eyes glazed over with greed as she reached out to touch it. There was only one problem . . .

"I'm Dominic," said Dominic, introducing himself.

"My, what a nice . . . hat," she said.

"It's mine!" said Dominic nervously. Having a thing about hats was one thing. Having a thing about *his* hat was something else . . .

Dominic is an ordinary boy who is mad for magic. Helping him is a very special hat, his magician's top hat – the Topper. But when Great Aunt Rowena comes to stay, Dominic discovers to his horror that his aunt is a Mad Hatter. And she wants the Topper . . .

Dominic Wood brings magic into the lives of millions with his TV shows. *Dom and the Magic Topper* is his first story for young readers.

www.kidsatrandomhouse.co.uk

Dominic Wood

Dom and the Magic Topper

With text by Pat Kelleher
Illustrated by Andy Hunt

DOM AND THE MAGIC TOPPER
A YOUNG CORGI BOOK : 9780552559034

First published in Great Britain by Young Corgi Books,
an imprint of Random House Children's Books

Young Corgi edition published 2004

Copyright © Dominic Wood, 2004
Illustrations copyright © Andy Hunt, 2004

The right of Dominic Wood to be identified as the author of this work has been
asserted in accordance with the Copyright, Designs and Patents Act 1988.

Set in Bembo Schoolbook by
Palimpsest Book Production Limited, Polmont, Stirlingshire

Young Corgi Books are published by Random House Children's Books,
61–63 Uxbridge Road, London W5 5SA,
A Random House Group Company

Addresses for companies within The Random House Group Limited
can be found at: www.randomhouse.co.uk/offices.htm

THE RANDOM HOUSE GROUP Limited Reg. No. 954009
www.**kids**at**randomhouse**.co.uk

A CIP catalogue record for this book is available from the British Library.

Printed and bound in Great Britain by
Cox & Wyman Ltd, Reading, Berkshire

To Mum and Dad.
Thanks for creating me –
I'm having a lovely time!

Chapter One

Dominic was an ordinary boy with
nothing up his sleeves
(except his arms). But
he was mad for magic.

His bedroom was full
of magic tricks.

He could tell you what
card you picked.

He could make coins
disappear.

He could wrap your
watch in a handkerchief,
smash it with
a hammer and it
would come out in

one piece again (well, most of the time).

About the only thing he couldn't do was saw somebody in half. And that was only because his dad kept the saw locked up in the garden shed. He told Dominic he didn't want to end up in the Sunday papers if it all went horribly wrong. He ought to make absolutely sure he knew exactly what

he was doing first. After all, there was no point in doing things by halves. But Dominic said that was *exactly* the point of sawing somebody in two.

And like any good magician
Dominic also had a Topper, a top hat.
Dominic had found it at a car boot
sale. Or at least he *thought* he found it.
Dominic had been browsing a stall looking for old magic sets when he saw something out of the corner of his eye. He was
sure it hadn't been there a moment earlier
but there it was. A top hat. Just what he
had wanted.

Looking back on it Dominic was never
quite sure whether *he* found the Topper, or
the *Topper* chose him. And if the Topper

knew, it wasn't telling. All Dominic knew for certain was that from that day to this, his life was filled with as much magic as he could handle, and then some.

Not that his parents seemed to notice.

"Mum, watch!" said Dominic one morning, pulling a spread of cards and a paper clip from the Topper. "I've got a  new card trick. Watch, Mum!"

"Not now, Dominic. I'm late for work. Show your father," said his mum flapping about, looking for her purse. Dominic's dad didn't work. Not since he lost his job at the factory. These days he rarely came out from behind his newspaper. Dominic's mum and dad didn't seem to have much magic left in their lives at all and didn't seem to notice it in anybody else's either.

"Dad, look!" exclaimed Dominic. "It's called 'Clipping the Jack'!"

"That's nice, son," said his dad, not even looking up from his paper. "Hmm. Says here that there was a fire at the Bulford Boarding Home. They're packing all the tenants off to relatives until they've redecorated. Isn't that where You-Know-Who lives?"

"If you mean my aunt Rowena," said Mum, "yes, it is."

"I have a Great Aunt Rowena?" said Dominic, looking up from his cards, astonished. It seemed he wasn't the only one who could pull things from thin air.

"Ah," said Dad. "Yes," he said, exchanging glances

with Mum, "but you haven't seen her since you were little. She's a little, well, eccentric."

"Eccentric?" said Dominic.

"She just has a thing, that's all," said Mum.

"A thing?" said Dominic. "What for?"

"Hats," said Dad solemnly.

"Hats?" said Dominic warily glancing at his own Topper.

"Yes, she's obsessed. She just can't stop collecting them. She spends all her money on them. She has quite a collection, by all accounts. Mind you, I expect she'll turn up here now, so you'll have a chance to see for yourself," said Dad.

"Well, we're the only relatives she's got," said Mum, having found her purse and realizing she was now late for work. "So if she does turn up look after her until I get home from work! And for goodness' sake don't laugh at her hats!" she warned as she left. "She's very touchy."

"I won't laugh at hers if she doesn't laugh at mine!" promised Dominic, patting the Topper on his head.

Chapter Two

Dominic may not have seen Great Aunt Rowena since he was little, but he knew her when he saw her. She was slim and elegant but her face had a hard edge that even layers of make-up and gold jewellery couldn't blunt. She stood at the door in an expensive designer jacket and skirt and the most outrageously strange, feathered hat Dominic had ever seen in his life. He wouldn't dare laugh at it even if he wanted to. It looked as if something bad-tempered and sullen had landed on her head and decided to roost there. And there was also the fact that she had a dozen slightly scorched hat

boxes with her. Dominic dreaded to think what was in *them*.

"Great Aunt Rowena!" he said.

Great Aunt Rowena sniffed, looking down her nose at Dominic. She didn't do children. But then she caught sight of the Topper on his head. Her eyes glazed over with greed as she reached out to touch it. There was only one problem . . .

"I'm Dominic," said Dominic, introducing himself.

"My, what a nice . . . hat," she said

"It's mine!" said Dominic nervously. Having a thing about hats was one thing. Having a thing about *his* hat was something else. And the Topper seemed to agree. Dominic could feel its brim tighten about his head, as if it was holding on for dear life. "I mean . . . it's my magic hat. That is, the hat I do magic tricks with," he added quickly. "It's not really magic. That would be silly," he said, "wouldn't it?"

Great Aunt Rowena stared hard at him and, for a moment, it looked as though she were going to snatch the hat from his head. But the moment passed. Great Aunt Rowena gave a haughty sniff and swept past him into the house leaving him to bring her boxes in and suitcases in. It looked as though she was planning to stay for a long time.

Dominic's eyes widened as she

reached up to her head and withdrew a long shiny hat-pin that had been holding her feathered hat in place before hanging the hat carefully on the hat stand in the hall.

"Derek," she said, crisply, to the newspaper.

"Rowena," said a voice curtly, from behind it.

There was a stony silence as Aunt Rowena perched tentatively on the edge of an armchair, as if she were afraid she might catch something if she sat in it properly. She looked around the room disdainfully, as if this were the last place she wanted to be.

Dominic finished stacking the last of the hatboxes in the hall with a clatter.

"Careful with those boxes. Their contents are priceless collectors' items. I've spent years amassing that collection. I won't have it ruined by one clumsy boy!" she snapped.

Dominic felt the Topper grip his head in anger.

"Ouch!" he hissed. "Stop it." The Topper relaxed its grip a little.

"So where's my niece?" asked Great Aunt Rowena impatiently.

"If you mean Mum," said Dominic, "she's working."

"Tut!" muttered Aunt Rowena, shooting a glance at the newspaper. "Most Right-Minded People don't approve of women going out to work," she added icily.

But Dominic knew how to break the ice. It was his speciality.

"Look, Great Aunt Rowena!" said Dominic, taking the Topper off and holding it in one hand. "Do you want to see a magic trick?" And with a grand flourish he produced a bouquet of flowers from it. He presented them to her. "Ta-daaaa!" He waited for the applause. He always got applause.

His Great Aunt blinked once. Twice.
Wrinkled up her nose and – "KHAGH-
TCHOOO!" The recoil from the sneeze
threw her back into the armchair. But
she didn't stop at one sneeze. In fact

 there seemed to
be no stopping
her at all. Dad
shrunk down
behind his
paper to wait
out the nasal
bombardment.
"I didn't
know she was
allergic to flowers!" he shouted over the
barrage of sneezes.

"But she can't be! They're artificial
flowers, special trick ones," called
Dominic, from behind the sofa where
he'd had taken cover with the Topper.

Great Aunt Rowena's sneezes began
to subside. And just in time. Dad's

newspaper had taken so many direct
hits it threatened to turn into papier
mâché at any moment. He went off to
the kitchen to see if he could salvage it.

Great Aunt Rowena flopped back in
the armchair, panting. She tried dabbing
her runny nose with a small, embroidered
lace hanky. It was clearly not up to the
job.

Dominic reached into the Topper and
plucked a large red handkerchief from
it. He offered it to her. "Um, there you
go, Great Aunt Rowena," he said. But it
only seemed to make her worse. She
broke out in a hideous, blotchy green
rash. Then she swelled up alarmingly.

And then (as if that wasn't enough) she started to sneeze again. And again.

Dominic offered her another hanky from the Topper. But this time, knotted to its corner, was another large handkerchief with another hanky knotted to that. "Ooops!" said Dominic as he pulled out hanky after hanky; great reams of reds, blues, greens and yellows not to mention the flags of all nations. There seemed to be no end to them. Dominic seemed as surprised as his great aunt did. "Stop it!" he hissed at the Topper, which seemed to be enjoying itself a little too much. And if you've ever seen a hat enjoying itself too much, you'll know what I mean.

Great Aunt Rowena glared at
Dominic with big, green puffy eyes.

"I thuppothe you think thads
funny?" she sniffled at the hankies piled
up round her feet. "Here I am thufferink
an' you're playink dricks!"

"I was only trying to help!"
exclaimed Dominic.

And that was when Mum came
home.

Chapter Three

"Aunt Rowena, what's happened?" cried Mum when she saw the state of her aunt.

"I didn't laugh at her hats, honest" said Dominic as he frantically stuffed the string of multicoloured hankies back into the Topper.

"Doh. He just laughed ab be!" said

 Great Aunt Rowena, glaring at him. Through sniffles and accusing looks Great Aunt Rowena explained about her sudden unexpected

allergy attack and how Dominic had
cheekily produced all those hankies from
his hat, as if it were all a big joke.

"But it wasn't like that at all!" said
Dominic in protest.

Great Aunt Rowena shot him an
angry glance.

"Is there anything I can do to help?"
asked Mum, fussing around her aunt.

"Well if you really want to be of
assistance, you can help me up to my
room. I feel all weak," said Great Aunt
Rowena ungratefully. "And bring my
hats," she said, twitching nervously. "I
must have my hats about me!"

So Mum helped Great Aunt Rowena
up to the
spare room.
She took
her great
feathered hat
up with her
as if she

couldn't bear to be parted from it. That left Dominic to struggle up the stairs with all her suitcases and hat boxes by himself.

Once Dominic had brought up the last hat box Great Aunt Rowena immediately made herself at home. She took to her bed and surrounded herself with her hats.

There was a straw sun hat, a boater, a bowler, a cashmere balaclava, several expensive sorts of hats festooned with ribbons, bows and things such as you might wear to weddings, a pillbox, a mortar board and a ten-gallon cowboy hat (or as it might be these days, a 44.5 litre hat).

Great Aunt Rowena's monstrous, feathered hat didn't so much hang on the bed post beside her, as *perch* on it. Her bright, shiny hat-pin lay on her bedside table. Having her hats round her seemed to make her feel calmer.

"I'm sure Dominic didn't mean anything by it," said Mum as she tucked her
in and plumped up her pillows. "I think
he was just trying to entertain you with
some magic, that's all."

"Magic?" spat Great Aunt Rowena.
"Trickery, more like. I don't approve of
prestidigitation. Most Right-Minded
People don't, you know. It's dishonest
and deceitful and it's practically the
same as lying!" she said.

Mum sighed. "I'll have a word with
him," she said.

"Perhaps you ought to confiscate that
hat of his. Teach him a lesson," she
urged. "Hats being used for playthings. I
never heard the like!"

"Well . . ." Mum began.

"I've got a nice strong hat box you could put it in," she offered, hopefully.

"I really don't think that's necessary," said Mum.

"We'll see," said Great Aunt Rowena, as if that settled the matter.

Downstairs Mum had a word with Dominic and Dad.

"She's had an allergic reaction to something, but I don't know what would bring her out in green blotches. We'll just have to be a little patient with her," said Mum. "She's obviously—"

"Round the twist?" said Dad, cracking his paper. He'd dried the sneeze-sodden paper off in the microwave and it was still a little bit crusty.

"I was going to say highly strung," said Mum.

24

"She's been eyeing up my hat," complained Dominic. "I bet she wants Topper for her collection!"

"Don't be silly," said his mum. "She was probably just admiring it, that's all."

But Dominic felt the Topper shudder in his hands and he tried to excuse himself from the room. "Er, I think I'll go upstairs and practise some magic," he said.

"Dom, love," Mum called after him. "I don't think you ought to do any magic while she's here. She has very

strong opinions about it. She's against it."

"But Mum!"

"No. No magic. We don't want to do anything else to upset her."

"Fine," sighed Dominic, who was now having a struggle to control the Topper in his hands. It was like trying to restrain an angry dog especially when

they had to creep quietly past Great Aunt Rowena's room to get to his own.

"Just great!" said Dom gloomily as he threw himself on his bed. "I find out I've got a Great Aunt Rowena I never knew I had – and now I wish I didn't. And what's with all that sneezing? I've never seen anybody sneeze like that before!"

A trumpet materialized out of the Topper and tooted a little fanfare. The Topper let out a loud sneeze and

ricocheted round the room before
landing back at Dominic's feet with a
somersault, like a dismounting gymnast.

It bowed trimphantly.
"Well, all right,"
said Dominic, "apart
from you, but you're
magic!" Slowly it
dawned on Dominic.

"That's it! That's what she's allergic
to! She's allergic
to you. To
magic!"

The Topper
cocked its brim
to one side,
quizzically.

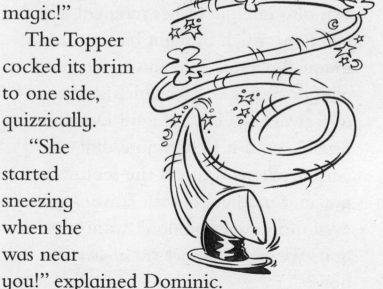

"She
started
sneezing
when she
was near
you!" explained Dominic.

"And went all blotchy and swollen when you started using your magic. She's allergic to magic!" he said.

"And because of your magic her allergic reaction was a magical one, that's why her blotches were green, not red.

And because she's allergic to magic she was also allergic to her magical allergic reaction, which brought her out in a magical allergic reaction to her magical allergic reaction – to which she was allergic, er, I think . . ." said Dominic dizzily. "And if I can figure that out, perhaps she can too. If she realizes you're a magical hat she'll want you even more and you don't want that, do you? We've got to get rid of her, but how?"

The Topper began to waddle slowly round in a circle, thinking. Then it stopped. There was a small puff of purple smoke and a piece of card shot out of it. Dominic caught it.

"An all-expenses-paid one-way ticket to China? I don't think you have to go that far," he said.

There was a rapping on the wall from his Great Aunt's room. "Keep the noise down, wretched boy, some of us are ill you know!" she snapped.

"On the other hand . . ." said Dominic.

Chapter Four

"Dinner time!" Mum called up the stairs some time later.

"Great, it's pizza and chips night. My favourite!" said Dominic. The Topper began to hop towards the door after him.

"No, you'd better stay up here," said Dominic. "If I'm right, Great Aunt Rowena's allergic to you and I don't want a repeat performance of this afternoon. The last thing I need is great-aunt-bogey topping on my pizza,

thank you very much. And besides," he added, "if she does want to add you to her collection, I think you'd better keep your head down."

The Topper sagged sulkily.

"You know what I mean. Stay out of her way. Don't let her see you," said Dominic as the Topper fidgeted. "Look, I won't be long," said Dominic with a 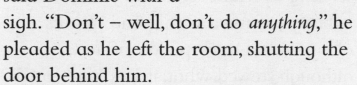 sigh. "Don't – well, don't do *anything*," he pleaded as he left the room, shutting the door behind him.

When Dominic entered the dining room Great Aunt Rowena was already there. She was slightly less green now and the swellings had gone down quite a bit, like a week-old party balloon; all soft and wrinkled. She went to the head of the table, where Dad usually sat, and sat down smartly in his place. Dad didn't say anything. He just shuffled along to a spare chair and sat down meekly. He looked over at Dominic and shrugged. At least it was pizza and chips night.

But it wasn't pizza and chips. Great Aunt Rowena had announced that Right-Minded People didn't hold with junk food. And she only agreed to come down when Mum promised to cook her favourite meal instead.

"It's the least you could do," she said selfishly as Mum served up plates of cabbage, mashed turnip and sprouts along with a thick puddle of stew, although stewed what, it was hard to tell.

Dominic looked at his plate. He wasn't fond of greens.

Dad looked at his plate. He wasn't fond of stew.

Mum just gave a weak smile as she sat down.

"Eat up. It builds character!" declared Great Aunt Rowena, tucking in. "And if you don't finish it you'll get it for breakfast tomorrow!"

Luckily, it was at times like these that Dominic found practising ordinary magic an advantage. With some well-practised sleight of hand he managed to palm several of the Brussels sprouts and drop them unseen into his trouser pockets.

Great Aunt Rowena domi-nated the

conversation throughout the meal (though never with her mouth full). In fact it wasn't so much a *conversation* – which requires that other people get to say things as well – it was more of a *speech*. She was very opinionated and gave her Right-Minded views on everything from how awful today's taxi drivers were to how tough prisons should be. And if you didn't believe the same then you weren't Right-Minded, and if you weren't Right-Minded you were quite simply . . . wrong. And you very probably didn't have a mind at all.

Dominic's parents were far too preoccupied to interrupt. They were too busy trying to digest the indigestible dinner.

Suddenly Dominic accidentally let

forth a loud sprouty burp.

Where there had only been the drone of Aunt Rowena's voice and the dutiful click and clatter of cutlery, there was now an awful silence.

Great Aunt Rowena glared at Dominic.

"Apologize at once!" she demanded.

"But I didn't do it on purpose," protested Dominic.

"Don't. Answer. Back," she said. "Most Right-Minded People believe children should be seen and not heard. And that bad manners should be punished."

When Mum and Dad said nothing, for fear of not appearing Right-Minded, Great Aunt Rowena took matters into her own hands. She slowly and deliberately dabbed her thin lips with her napkin then pointed sharply to the dining-room door.

"Go to your room," she demanded. "And you won't be getting any supper, either!"

"But we don't have su—"
"Ah."
"But we—"
"Ah-ah."
Dominic looked at his mum and dad for help, but they just shrugged and stared glumly at their plates.

Great Aunt Rowena folded her arms

and watched him with her beady eyes as he sloped moodily off to his bedroom.

"It's so unfair!" he said gloomily as he flicked playing cards into the Topper. No magic. No pizza. No fun. Everything had changed since Great Aunt Rowena had arrived.

Dominic flicked another card. It missed – but the Topper jumped and caught it.

Down below, in the dining room, Dominic could hear Great Aunt Rowena talking again. He pressed his ear to the floor, but couldn't make anything out.

"I'm sure she's talking about me," he said with a frown. "I wish I could hear what she was saying."

The Topper suddenly leaped into the
air, performed a somersault and collapsed
down towards its brim like a sinking
soufflé, until it was a flattened disc.

"I didn't realize you were a collapsible
top hat, Topper!" said Dominic.

The flattened Topper
landed on the floor. It
was as if someone
had cut a circular
hole in the floor
surrounded by a
hat brim. Dominic
peered down
through the magical
hole and could see right into
the dining room below. There, just under
the lampshade directly beneath him, he
could see Great Aunt Rowena eating
her favourite dessert – prunes and
custard.

"That boy needs taking in hand,"
she was saying. "He's far too wilful.

And as for that hat of his! Why, any
Right-Minded Person can see that hat
is obviously an object of exquisite
craftsmanship and history. In fact I
suspect it's a hat of great worth. Of
course, I'd need to inspect it properly to
be sure, but it could be quite valuable.
A collector's item, in fact."

The Topper positively glowed with pride.

"And as such I think it would be better off in my possession. As one who knows about the proper care and appreciation of millinery, I'm sure you'll agree that I'm right."

"Well—" said Dominic's mum in a small voice.

Holding his breath Dominic leaned forward to listen more closely. As he did so a Brussels sprout fell out of his pocket, bounced across the floor and dropped though the Topper-hole before he could catch it. It landed in Great Aunt Rowena's bowl of prunes and custard with a *SPLAT!*

"What on earth—" spluttered Great Aunt Rowena and started to look up.

Dominic gasped, lurched back and ripped the Topper off the floor. The hole vanished. The floor was solid again.

Dominic smacked the Topper with the palm of his hand and it snapped back into its full shape.

"Phew!" he sighed. "That was a lucky escape!"

The Topper nodded its brim in agreement.

"No, not that. I mean prunes and custard for afters – yuk!"

But then he heard the sound of foot-steps coming upstairs. They clomped along the landing and stopped outside his room.

Quickly Dominic put the Topper on his bedside table and hopped on the bed, as if he had been there for ages. He tried very hard to look as innocent as possible.

The door handle turned. Great Aunt
Rowena peered round the door and
gazed around his room at the stacks of
old, well–used magic sets, the shelves of
magic books, the assortment of boxes,
balls, trick cups, packs of marked cards

and other magical props as if it confirmed her worst fears. Her gaze alighted on the Topper before flicking to Dominic. She stared at him.

"I don't know how you managed that – that prank with the sprout," she said in controlled fury, "but if anything like that happens again, I shall make sure all this," and here she gestured round the room to the magical paraphernalia, "all this will – will—"

But as she spoke her face began to take on a greenish tinge. Her nose began to crinkle, her cheeks began to twitch. She shut the door quickly. There was a moment's silence and then the landing echoed to a loud *KHAGH-CHOOOO!*

"And I don't wod doo hear a beeb owd of you," she hissed back through the door. "I like my sleep!"

And, as if to make sure she wouldn't be disturbed, Dominic heard her lock his bedroom door.

Chapter Five

If Great Aunt Rowena had expected
Dominic to panic or make a fuss she
was disappointed. Dominic wasn't in the
slightest bit worried about being locked
in his bedroom. He was a magician
after all.

"If I need to get out I can always
practise my escapology skills," he said
with a grin. And
even if they failed,
well, he had a
magic Topper,
didn't he? So he just
got ready for bed
and went to sleep.

But Great Aunt Rowena didn't sleep.

She had a plan.

In the middle of the night she unlocked Dominic's bedroom door and opened it. Wearing her cashmere balaclava hat over her head, Great Aunt Rowena slipped quietly into the room. Dominic was fast asleep and the Topper was slumped to one side in a snooze.

She carefully lifted up the Topper from the bedside cabinet and slipped out of the room again, forgetting, in her excitement, to lock the door behind her.

Back in the safety of her room, she took off her disguise. She turned the Topper round in her hands, inspecting it closely, stroking it and caressing it.

"Such workmanship, such elegance, such millinery!" she exclaimed. "Much too good for a little boy!" She put it down on the chest of drawers so she could admire it. "Well, you're my hat now!" she said. "And I've prepared a special hat box just for you!" She started to unbuckle the strong leather straps on a reinforced, padded hat box.

Alarmed by the sound, the Topper awoke and leaped back off the chest of drawers out of her clutches.

Great Aunt Rowena gasped in

 surprise. "Oh, you're even more special than I could ever have imagined!" she said. "You shall be my Special Hat. My Very Special Hat! Now I have you

I don't need my other hats at all!"

The Topper backed away, but found itself cornered over by the wardrobe.

"Oh no, you don't," Rowena hissed, reaching out for it.

The Topper shrank away from her, almost as if it were afraid. Then – *POP!* It fired a magical, glowing bubble into the air. It arced over Great Aunt Rowena's head.

"Missed!" she gloated.

But the Topper hadn't been aiming for

her. The bubble burst over the hats lying on the bed. It showered them with a twinkling dust. As it settled over them they started to twitch.

Then they started to move.

The misshapen, monstrous hats
slipped off the bed. They began to limp
and shuffle across the room towards
their mistress. If the hats weren't revolt-
ing before they certainly were now.
Together they were making a stand
against her. A last, desperate hat stand.
It was a fearsome sight. The rustle of
raffia, the slither of silk and the soft
flop of twisted felt filled the room as the
militant millinery advanced towards her.

"No!" she gasped. "Stop it! Stay back. I'm your owner. Your mistress! Back! Back, I say!"

Who knows what terrible crimes you can commit against hats? Or maybe they just overheard her saying that she didn't need them any more. But, whatever it was, they didn't seem too happy with her. The Topper watched as the hats cornered Great Aunt Rowena against the wall, surrounding her, pressing in closer and closer.

"Get away!" she squealed, trying to stomp on them with her feet. Slowly she began to turn green and blotchy again – because her hats were alive and magic was everywhere.

"Traitors!" she squealed as they began to form a ring round her. The Topper hopped back onto the chest of drawers to direct the battle.

Great Aunt Rowena made a grab at her bedside table and snatched up her hat-pin. She thrust and poked the pin wildly about her trying to drive back the advancing horde of hats, tearing at ribbons, ripping at bows and fraying frills.

Only Great Aunt Rowena's monstrous feathered hat hadn't yet turned against her. It sat watching from its bedpost perch. Now, with a squawk, it took off

and flew unsteadily round the room on stunted, misshapen feathered wings.

"Squwaark!" it cried, swooping down at Great Aunt Rowena, harrying her, snatching at her hair before finding a perch on top of the wardrobe.

"Squwaark! Traitors?" it cried in a high parroty voice as if it wasn't used to using it. "Traitors? Not us! *You* are the one who has betrayed us. Betrayed hatkind! All we ever  wanted to be was hats, to be worn on a head with love and pride, to be shown off. Squwaark! To go to a few weddings, an Easter Parade even."

Great Aunt Rowena flung an empty hat box at it in desperation, but missed.

The feathered hat flapped over to the dressing table where Topper stood and continued its rant.

"Squwaark! But no greater cruelty can you show to hats than to keep us locked up unworn and hidden away in musty, old boxes."

"No, it's not true!" said Great Aunt Rowena. "Hats are the only thing in my life. They *are* my life," she panted as she jabbed unsuccessfully with the hat-pin.

"I wore *you!*" she spat.

"Squwaark! Fastened with a pin so there was no escape. *That* pin!" It squawked and swooped down, snatched the pin  from her hands and dropped it triumphantly down behind the wardrobe. "My feathers once belonged to a bird and have a memory of freedom, but since I was made I've been restrained by pin and box. But nevermore! Now I can be *free*. Now we can *all* be free of you, thanks to the Topper!"

"No, never! If I can't have you, no one can!" hissed Great Aunt Rowena.

But before she could do anything about it, her face screwed up. Her nose wrinkled, twitched, then exploded in an enormous sneeze.

Chapter Six

In his bedroom Dominic sat up with a start, woken by Great Aunt Rowena's sneeze.

"But she only sneezes when she's near the Topper," he said blearily. He looked over at his bedside cabinet. It was empty!

He grabbed his wand and dashed into the spare room. The sight that met his eyes astounded him. The hats were swarming round his great aunt. The monstrous feathered hat was flapping round the room, squawking like an agitated parrot. And the Topper was in the thick of it, hopping round her, whirling a lasso above its brim. It threw

the loop over Great Aunt Rowena's head. It dropped down over her arms. The Topper hopped back, pulling the lasso tight, pinning her arms to her side. But it didn't stop her stomping on the hats.

Dominic knew he had to help. He had an idea. He whistled to the Topper. The Topper turned. It left the lasso and jumped up. Dominic caught it. Then, with a sharp smack, he collapsed the Topper, flattening it into a disc which he then threw at the wall. It stuck and started to glow. The Topper had become a magical portal again. Dominic peered through

the Topper-hole in the wall. He could
see right through it into the garden
below. Now he had to save the Topper's
fellow hats from a millinery massacre.

"This way! Quick!" he called to the
other hats. Under cover of another of
Great Aunt Rowena's sneezing attacks,
they scuttled as quickly as they could
towards the Topper-hole. The feathered
hat swooped down on Great Aunt
Rowena to distract her and buy them a
few more precious moments.

"Go! Go! Go!" cried Dominic ushering
the other hats through the Topper-hole
like a parachute instructor.

Led by the balaclava, they hopped through it down into the night and to freedom, dragging their frayed and trampled companions with them. At the last moment the feathered hat tucked in its wings and with a final "Squwaark!" it dived through the portal and was gone.

Dominic saw the renegade hat band scurry off into the shrubbery at the bottom of the garden. A bowler hat turned back for one last glance, tipped itself politely in Dominic's direction – and then that, too, was gone.

Dominic peeled the Topper off the wall and the hole vanished. With a quick slap against the heel of his hand Dominic

popped the Topper back to its proper
shape. He barely had time to wonder
how a pack of wild hats might survive
out there before he heard a strangled
cry. Great Aunt Rowena had wriggled
free of the lasso. He threw himself to the
floor as a crazed Great Aunt Rowena,
her hair hanging untidily around her
face, leaped at him. As he
fell the Topper
slipped from
his grasp.

Great Aunt
Rowena
snatched it
up. Holding
it tightly, so
it couldn't escape,
she placed it triumphantly on her head.

"You may have taken my hats from
me, but at least I have this one!" she said.

Dominic looked up in horror. His
Topper!

"It's my hat-*CHOOO!* now!" sneezed his great aunt, standing over him. She gave the Topper a pat as if to jam it on her own head even more tightly. But the Topper had one last trick up its sleeve. It slipped right down over her head as if it had suddenly become two sizes too big. Great Aunt Rowena tugged at the brim of the Topper.

"Get off! Get. Off!" Dominic heard her muffled voice from inside the Topper as he scrambled to his feet. But. It. Just. Wouldn't. Budge. Then suddenly — with a pop — it came off. But now Great Aunt Rowena had TWO heads!

Both alike, both just as mean and nasty – but only one was green and blotchy.

Great Aunt Rowena looked at herself. Great Aunt Rowena looked back. She was still holding the Topper tightly in her hands. But now she had two heads they couldn't decide which one should get to wear it. Great Aunt Rowena began to argue with herself, tugging the Topper from left to right.

"It's my hat!" she said.

"No, it's mine!" she said back.

The two heads glared at each other.

"It's mine!" they said together.

"No, it's mine!" they snapped back.

Then the green and blotchy head threw itself back and sneezed. The Topper shot out of Great Aunt Rowena's hands.

"Now look what you've done!" cried her other head.

"Wad!?" sniffled the green, blotchy head, turning to glare at her and accidentally sneezing all over her other head.

"Why you—"

But Great Aunt Rowena's green, blotchy head couldn't hear over the sneezes. The other head, being magic, wasn't allergic to the Topper's magic and didn't sneeze at all. Dominic wondered, since the second head was magic, too, if the green, blotchy head was allergic to *that* as well.

Dominic left them to it. He took the Topper and tiptoed back to his room. "She will return to normal, won't she?" asked Dominic in hushed tones.

The Topper just shrugged its brim.

Dominic could still hear his Great Aunt Rowenas (or should that be *Aunts* Rowena?) arguing with each other as he drifted back off to sleep, his Topper safely on his bedside cabinet again.

Chapter Seven

The next morning Dominic went down to breakfast half expecting to see last night's dinner served up again.

But there was no sign of cold stew or Great Aunt Rowena. He sat anxiously at the breakfast table to eat his cereal and put the Topper down on the table beside him. It seemed quite happy with itself, if not a little bit smug. Dad was

CHAT Sport
Daily Chat

HAT SEEN CATCHING BUS TO HATFIELD

SUPPORTERS HAT GETS WINNING GOAL FOR CITY.

RARE BIRD SPOTTED EYE WITNESS SAID "IT LOOKED JUST LIKE A HAT..."

WHEATI CHUR

behind his paper and Mum was rushing
about, getting ready for work as usual.
Dominic heard Great
Aunt Rowena
coming down
the stairs.

"Oh no, here she comes," he
whispered to the Topper.
What if she still had two heads? How
would he explain that? Would she tell his
parents everything? Would she blame him
for the loss of her priceless hat collection?
Great Aunt Rowena appeared in the
doorway. She was dressed and ready to

go out. She looked twice as frightful as she had done the night before, probably because she had been up all night arguing with herself, but to Dominic's relief she only had one head again. But which head was it? The real one, or the magical one? He couldn't tell, and if the Topper could, it wasn't giving anything away.

Great Aunt Rowena stared anxiously at the Topper as if it were going to jump up and swallow her whole.

"I can't stay here," she said in a quavery voice. "There's obviously something in this house I'm allergic to. Cats or dust or . . ."

"Common sense?" muttered Dad behind his paper

". . . So I won't stay a moment longer! I'm leaving," declared Great Aunt Rowena.

"But Aunt Rowena, said Mum. "I know we got off to a bad start, but—"

"No, my mind's made up," she

protested. "I can't stay in a house with – with things like that!" she said, pointing a slightly green and trembly finger at the Topper.

"But I thought you liked hats," said Mum, puzzled.

"No!" shrieked Great Aunt Rowena. "I never want to see another hat as long as I live!" she said as she stormed out of the house. "I much prefer . . . *gloves*!"

And as she slammed the door behind
her Dominic thought
he saw in her coat
pocket a pair of
his mum's best
leather gloves.
"Don't try
and stop
me!" called
Great Aunt
Rowena as
she dashed
down the
path, vowing
never to come
back.

And nobody did.

"Well! What do you make of that?"
said Mum thoughtfully.

"Mad as a hatter," said Dad, from
behind his newspaper.

As Mum hurried off to work, and
Dad turned to the sports section,

Dominic could feel the Topper quake ominously in his hands. He excused himself and hurried up to his room. And just in time. As he shut the door, the Topper went off, firing party poppers, streamers and party blowers all over the room to celebrate getting rid of Great Aunt Rowena, the Mad Hatter.

"You know," said Dominic, after the Topper had finished doing a victory dance round the room. "For a hat, you can be awfully big-headed!"

Hat's All, Folks!

CLIPPING THE JACK

Want to be a magician like Dominic?

Why not try Dominic's *Clipping The Jack* trick? You don't need a magic Topper to make it work. It's a simple trick that will easily fool your friends.

You will need:

Five old playing cards: four black suit cards with high numbers like the *Ten of Clubs* or the *Nine of Spades* and one red suit Jack, either the *Jack of Hearts* or the *Jack of Diamonds*.

A glue stick.

A large paper clip

Instructions

Arrange the cards in a row with their
edges overlapping, as shown in the
picture. They should be spaced out so
that they overlap by about 1.5cm.
Make sure the Jack is in the centre.
Now glue them together.

The Trick

Show the row of cards face up to a friend. Ask them to remember where the Jack is then turn the cards over so they are face down.

Now give the friend the paper clip and ask them to mark the Jack by clipping the paper clip onto it. They'll place the clip on the middle card.

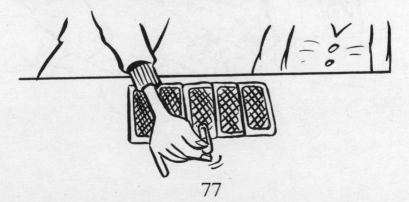

When they've done this turn the cards back over to reveal that their paper clip is, in fact, nowhere near the Jack! They'll be astonished and won't know how you've done it.

How It Works

You haven't *actually* done anything. The trick is really a simple optical illusion that deceives the eyes and fools the brain – if you don't give people too long to think about it!

Dominic Wood

CHECK OUT THESE BRILLIANT MAGIC BOOKS BY DOMINIC WOOD:

Dominic Wood's Magic Book

A Bodley Head hardback

0 370 32756 X

Red Fox paperback

0 099 447697 3

Spooky Magic

A Bodley Head hardback

0 370 32766 7

Simply Magic

Red Fox paperback

0 099 41396 5

Playground Pranks

AMAZING MAGIC IN MOMENTS!

Make break time fun with these
pocket-sized playground pranks.
Amaze your friends and impress the
teachers with stunning magical feats.

With handy photos, clear step-by-step
instructions and the simplest of props,
you can be the most popular kid in school.

Red Fox paperback 0 099 45138 7

Party Tricks

AMAZING MAGIC IN MOMENTS!

Impress your friends with these pocket-sized party tricks and take centre stage to wow and wonder with your amazing magic skills.

With handy photos, clear step-by-step instructions and the simplest of props, you too can be the life and soul of the party.

Red Fox paperback 0 099 45137 9

All Random House Children's
Books titles are available

By phone: 01624 677237

By post:
Random House Children's Books
c/o Bookpost, PO Box 29
Douglas, Isle of Man, IM99 11Q

By fax: 01624 670923

By email: bookshop@enterprise.net

Cheques (payble to Bookpost)
and credit cards accepted

Prices and availabiity subject
to change without notice.

Allow 28 days for delivery

Free Post and Packing
Overseas customers allow
£2.00 per paperback

When placing your order, please mention if you
do not wish to receive additional information.

www.kidsatrandomhouse.co.uk